ANNA

The Watcher

BASED ON
THE MAN ON THE MOON

PROLOGUE
DRALRAN

FIVE HUNDRED YEARSS AGO

I thrust one final time into the warm pussy shrouding my dick in its decadent juices and grunt my release, deep.

"Fuck." I collapse down onto the sweaty body that owns the pussy. "Fucking heaven."

"I doubt it's heaven, Dral. After all, I'm the Devil's daughter. You mean it's perfect hell."

"Heaven or hell. You've milked me of everything I can give."

"Damn, I was hoping for a repeat performance."

The little minx pushes me away, and my dick slides from her pussy. Lilith is as insatiable as I am when it comes to exploits in the bedroom. This isn't a relationship—we're fuck buddies. I don't pretend for one minute that when she leaves me she's not going to be opening her legs for someone else. She's all about getting as much power behind her as she can, and seduction is her favored method because it kills two birds with one stone. She can get sexual satisfaction while at the same time build an army.

I'm not exactly faithful either. She's the third woman I've slept with today. My sex drive is incredibly high, and I have to keep myself satisfied or my balls swell to the size of melons. Well, that's a bit of an exaggeration, but they definitely feel like they do. When you're more than two hundred years old and in the Devil's employment, there's little else to do other than torture people or have sex.

My specialty is fire. The souls drifting down here from Earth are subject to my fiery brand of purgatory. It's the best fun a demon can have, but lately I've been feeling more and more jaded—hence the increased time spent in the company of willing women like Lilith. Sex is the only thing that seems to entertain me at the moment. The novelty of burning flesh from bones has worn off. Ever since I went to Earth and walked around it for a few days while on a task for Satan, I've longed for something different.

I let out a sigh and relax back on the bed, my arm hooked under my head, watching as Lilith dresses.

"Well, if you're not going to spend the rest of the evening buried balls deep in me, I'd better go and find someone who will."

"I didn't say that."

"Even three times in a day is a bit much for you, Dral," Lilith teases me, and I pull her toward me. She's covered her breasts in a bra, but her pussy is still bare. I sniff.

"Seems three times is not enough for you, though. That's not just my scent here, is it?" I drag my finger through her folds.

"Jealous?" She smirks sinfully.

"Nope. Not in the slightest." I effortlessly pull her back over me and slide her onto my already hard dick. "We both know who the best lover is."

"Cocky much?"

I laugh playfully.

"We both know my dick is the biggest you've had."

"It'll also be the last dick she has, if I have my way, but needs must..." A mysterious voice fills the air, and a flash of smoke floods the room before Lilith's father appears. Satan himself—eyes as black as the night and a full three piece suit to match. The only glimpse of color on him is the blood-red cuff links holding his shirt in place.

Shit!

Caught balls deep in his daughter.

This will not end well.

"Get off his dick, Lilith, and go home. Wash yourself thoroughly. I better not smell any demons on you when I get back. You're meeting your future husband tonight."

"Dad!" Lilith goes to protest, but smoke surrounds her father again—a sign of the fury dwelling within him. "Fine." Lilith moves from the bed and collects the rest of her clothing. "I'm not marrying anyone ugly. You promised me."

"I'm the Devil, darling. I don't have to keep promises. Now *go.*"

Lilith disappears from the room in her own flash of smoke. I've got the same ability to teleport but not with such flair. That's reserved for the royal family alone. I make to slide from the bed, but a growl from the Devil freezes me in position with my dick on display.

"I'm a little disappointed in you, Dralran. You're one of my best demons, but here I find you sleeping with my daughter. I wouldn't expect such disloyalty from you, even if she is a whore to most of the kingdom."

"I'm sorry, my liege." I try to move and cover myself again, but the Devil sets fire to my underwear before I can put them on. The rest of the clothes I'd discarded on my bedroom floor meet the same fate. Am I next?

"You know what disappoints me the most—it's your commitment to the underworld. You've changed, Dralran. You were one of my best torturers, but these days, I'm more likely to find you buried deep in a woman than setting fire to a condemned soul before reviving them and then repeating the process for years and years. What's happened?"

I'm standing up now and place my hands over my groin area. It's a little uncomfortable being in this position in front of my employer, especially with my dick covered in the aftermath of his daughter's orgasm.

"I don't know, my liege. I've felt strange since I visited Earth. I saw so much I didn't know before. It captured my imagination, and I liked it."

"You liked the humans?" Satan flicks a fire arrow at my feet, and I dance around the sparks. He sends another, so I immediately skip back the other way.

"Not the humans necessarily, but the way they interact and how they're development is so far behind ours. Horses are their only mode of transport. It seems odd when we can think of a place and be there."

More arrows have me dancing, hopping from one foot to the other, the entire time I'm replying.

"Hmm." The Devil is disappointed in me. I can see it in his eyes. He stops launching arrows at me and rubs his chin. "You like to watch?"

"No, I like my job. It's been in my family for generations. There's nothing better than torturing your souls."

"Except fucking my daughter?" Satan raises a questioning eyebrow at me.

"Ok, that's better, but no, I didn't mean sex. Shit!" I'm getting flustered, and it will result in me ending up in a smoking pile of ash on the floor.

"You've lost your way, and I can't allow it to continue. I must teach you a lesson."

"I'm sorry." I lower my head and prepare for my death. This is the Devil—you don't argue with him when he makes a proclamation. It's futile.

The scenery around us changes, and I'm confused when I look up and see I'm in space. The Earth is illuminated by the Sun in front of me as I stand on the rough surface of the Moon.

"What's happening?"

"Dralran, for sleeping with my daughter, I hereby banish you to the Moon. You want to watch the Earth, then watch it."

A flash of smoke surrounds the Devil, and he disappears.

I try to teleport back to Hell, but nothing happens. Again and again I try, but I'm stuck here. A few seconds later, boxes appear out of nowhere. When I open them, I discover they contain my belongings.

He wasn't joking. I really am banished here, alone for all eternity.

CHAPTER ONE
EMMA

PRESENT DAY.

"Come on, Emma. Hurry up, or we'll miss it," my best friend calls as we race toward the bus stop, jumping over puddles of water left by the torrential downpour earlier.

We could easily walk the short distance to the Greenwich Observatory, but neither of us is in the mood to risk getting drenched with more rain forecast before an evening of clear skies. I can't wait to look up at the Moon and stars again if the clouds do clear. I'm not a Heaven and Hell kind of person, I'm more of a 'we'll all become stars' believer. Since my parents died in a car crash when I was fifteen years old, it's the one thing keeping me slightly sane. Knowing I could be looking up at them twinkling in the sky.

"Emma, come on." Leah jumps onto the bus, and I follow her.

We both tap our credit cards against the card machine to pay our fare and then find a seat. It only takes five minutes to get to our destination, and we both hop off together, saying thank-you to our driver.

"I'm really going to try looking for Venus tonight. It's supposed to be in perfect alignment, and the closest it's been in years," my friend says excitedly.

Leah works at the UK space agency in Swindon, and often when she comes to visit me, we go to the Greenwich Observatory, especially if it's one of the special evenings when you can look through the Great Equatorial Telescope. Tonight is one of those occasions.

I'm sometimes envious of her job. It would have been something I'd like to have done if I had the chance. My life took a different path, though. I wouldn't say it was a bad one. I do love my job, but sometimes, I long for more excitement—something more out of this world.

When my parents died, I was sent to stay with my aunt on my father's side. She wasn't really impressed at having a hormonal fifteen-year-old thrust upon her, especially as she'd lived most of her life as a fun-loving spinster. It took us a while to find a rhythm between us. We eventually got there, but not in enough time for me to get the exam results I needed to go to college with Leah. Instead, I followed my other passion, drawing, and eventually I was lucky enough to receive an apprenticeship with a popular artist in London. I've been helping him and developing my own style ever since. I had my first exhibition last year and sold most of my pieces. I'm already planning another one later this year.

"This queue is going to take forever." Leah sighs as we join the relatively small line, in my eyes anyway. I've seen it a lot longer than this before.

"You're so impatient."

"It's the busy city life. I'm used to living in the countryside now." She giggles.

Leah and I have been friends since I moved in with my aunt. She lived next door, and we bonded over the garden fence. We gave her parents and my aunt nightmares when, at eighteen, we started driving to concerts and going out into town with other friends and boys. The boys part infuriated my aunt as they tended to flock around me like lost sheep. I didn't think I was anything special, but apparently my slight build, long brown hair, and chestnut eyes mixed with my pert size 'C' boobs captured their attention. The fact I liked short skirts probably helped as well. I've grown up a bit since then. Jeans and tops, normally covered in paint, are more my fashion choice now although my boobs still capture their fair share of attention.

"I'd miss the noise of the city if I wasn't in it."

Having moved up to the first position in the queue, we're both standing against the wall with our arms folded over our chests, trying to keep ourselves warm.

"You get different noises such as birds singing, and things like that."

I look up at the sky. The clouds have cleared now, and the stars are shining down at me.

"What does space sound like?" I ask.

Leah looks up as well.

"Space is a vacuum. Sounds aren't the same as they are here on Earth. That doesn't mean there aren't any—they're just different, and often they're eerie. There's a YouTube video of them. I'll send you the link."

"Thanks," I reply as we're ushered into the observatory room.

We have ten minutes to look through the telescope before it's someone else's turn. Leah goes first, and I know she's homing in on exactly where Venus should be. She twists and turns the dials trying to get a decent picture.

"There you are." She wiggles her bottom excitedly when she finds Venus.

"Let me have a look." I push her aside and peer through the telescope to the burning planet. "Wow!" I exclaim.

"I'll be back in a minute. I just want to ask the guide a question," Leah tells me.

"Ok," I reply.

As I've still got some time left, I turn the telescope around and see what else I can observe. The Moon comes into view. It's always fascinated me and not just because of the rumors about it being made of cheese, which happens to be my favorite food. I've always found it intriguing because of how barren it is, and yet vitally important to the Earth. I adjust the dials to focus better and scan the rocky surface.

My hands freeze on the dials when I see a man standing there. He's wearing jeans and a t-shirt, and his long brown hair falls around his shoulders. He waves and mouths,

"Hi, Emma."

I step back from the telescope and rub my eyes

before looking through it once more. He's still there, and he waves at me again.

"Er...Leah," I call my friend back over.

"What's up? You look pale."

"Look through the telescope. What do you see?"

"Should I be worried?"

She bends down and looks into the eyepiece.

"It's the Moon."

"Just the Moon?" I push her out the way again and stare up into space.

The man shakes his head at me and mouths, *"Our secret."*

"Times up," the guide calls, and Leah ushers me away from the telescope.

When we get outside, I look up to the Moon is, but even though it's full and relatively close to the Earth, I can't see anything…or anyone.

"Are you ok?" Leah looks at me in concern.

"Yeah." I nod. "I think I've been working too hard this week. I need to relax. Let's go and get something to eat."

"Good idea."

Sometime later, having eaten, Leah and I return to my flat and have a couple of drinks before she heads to bed. Knowing we'll be having a long day tomorrow, shopping until we drop, I retire as well and fall instantly into a deep sleep.

I'm lying on my bed in the middle of a barren wasteland. To my left and right, there's nothing but mist. It's then he appears, the man from the Moon. He's still wearing his jeans, but he's lost his t-shirt, and I can't help noticing the muscular sculpture of his body, which is covered in tattoos of different symbols I don't recognize. My breath hitches, and my lungs are unable to fill with air on seeing the delicious sight in front of me.

"*You were a bad girl trying to get Leah to see me. It doesn't work that way. I'm your demon on the Moon.*"

"*I don't understand. How were you there? Here? I mean...who are you?*"

"*I'm the Watcher.*"

Without another word, the man lowers himself down my body. As my eyes follow him, I realize I'm naked. I try to cover myself up, but I can't because me hands are now tied to the bed.

"*What are you going to do?*" *I ask in desperation, but the man doesn't answer.*

Instead, he parts my legs and dips his head between them. Next thing I know, his tongue traces the length of my slit. I arch my back off the bed as he continues to feast on my pussy. I don't even know his name, yet he's eating me like I'm his last meal ever. My body ignites, all nerves pounding with feelings of desire.

"Please," I whimper lustfully, needing more.

I'm rewarded with a finger inserted into my pussy, followed by another. I feel full, but it's bliss.

"Such a good girl, really," the man murmurs against my clit, and his warm breath tantalizes the already sensitive bud. "Perfect under my body. I can't wait to fuck you, hard and long. All night as you stare up at the stars."

I know I should be scared of his words because I saw him standing on the fucking moon earlier, for Christ's sake, but I'm not. I'm too far gone under his expert handling of my body to care.

The orgasm bursts from deep within my core and rapidly travels all around my body before landing back where it began. I can't stop shaking, groaning, and wanting more from the man between my thighs.

He withdraws his fingers and licks them while sitting back up.

"Delicious," he moans around his fingers, his own voice full of lust. "It's going to be perfect."

"Perfect?" I question, unsure of what he means, but I don't receive an answer.

He disappears, and the fog returns, cascading around me.

CHAPTER TWO
DRALRAN

I long for the real touch of her, but all I can manage at the moment is to project into her dreams. It's cruel. Surely I've learned my lesson by now. Five hundred years on the Moon is far too long. Lilith is happily married now with several children, so it's not like I'm going to be sleeping with her ever again, even if I wanted to, which I don't. I've been captured by Emma's beauty, and I'll never look at another woman again, but she's aging fast. Soon she'll be gone, and I'll still be stuck here on the Moon...for eternity.

A thought hits me.

A plan even.

It could work.

I still have my magic.

Just not my ability to teleport.

I have to taste her for real.

To know her scent.

Her flavor.

"Bakoth!" I call, looking down at Hell where my friend is currently entertaining a pretty banshee. I entertained her a few times myself before I was trapped here, but she's nothing in comparison to Emma. "I need you." Bakoth continues to fuck the banshee. "Now," I add urgently.

Bakoth pulls out and shakes his fist at me. He's visited me regularly since I've been up here, bringing me the things I need. The Devil knows about the arrangement. He doesn't mind Bakoth getting me food and supplies because even though, under its surface, the Moon is full of cheese, there's only so much a demon can eat before he goes insane and gets the mother of all migraines. However, the Devil did ban Bakoth from bringing me demon women after the first time I asked for one.

A few minutes later, Bakoth appears.

"What?" he growls angrily.

"I need your help."

"What do you need?" The big man folds his arms across his chest.

"I want you to fetch me a woman."

He groans, annoyed I brought him up here for this again.

"The Devil says I can't bring you a woman. I'm not going against him—I like my life as it is. Food and supplies only."

I smirk knowingly.

"No, the Devil said you can't bring me a demon woman. He didn't mention anything about a human woman."

"What the…" Bakoth's mouth drops open. "I can't do that for you. It would expose us to the humans."

I chuckle playfully.

"We're already exposed to the humans in so many ways. For God sake, they tell stories about me on Earth—they call me the Man in the Moon. And you're known for those weird crop circle designs you make in the fields."

"Humans are so stupid! They always blame aliens for those when, in reality, the only thing aliens are responsible for is bringing hot dogs to Earth. They know nothing."

Bakoth shakes his head.

"Seriously though, Dralran, you know I'd do anything for you, but I can't do this. If Satan finds out, he'll burn my balls off and feed them to his dogs.

I'd like to give my mum little demon grandchildren one day."

I slump back against the makeshift house I've made. It's on the dark side of the Moon so the humans can't see it with their telescopes.

"Please, Bakoth. It's not part of the rules, and I'll keep her here with me. She won't be returning to Earth, so she can't tell anyone. Hundreds of people go missing on Earth every day without a trace—most of them stumbling onto something they shouldn't. I've watched her since the day she was born. She's mine. I know it in my heart, and I long to touch her and feel her under me. Please."

"Fuck, you do have it desperate."

Bakoth wrinkles his nose up.

"Maybe I do. Have you ever wanted something so bad you can't give up on it, no matter what?"

"I always crave chili coated donuts."

"Imagine Hell is full of them, but you're not allowed to eat them. That's how I feel."

"Man, that would suck."

I start to walk around to the lighter side of the Moon where the Earth is illuminated by the sun. Bakoth follows me, and we both look down. Emma is walking to work. She's in tatty overalls, and I know she'll be painting all day. She's got a picture to finish.

Ironically, it's an image of the Moon. I can't help wondering whether I'll be added into it in some way now.

I take in her long brown hair pulled up into a messy bun, and her mocha eyes. You can't tell from the overalls she's wearing, but her body is stunning underneath. She's got curves in all the right places and a fabulous pair of tits. I need her here with me. I'm a selfish bastard, but I have to taste her.

"There she is." I point her out to Bakoth.

"She's pretty," he responds.

"See why I want her here with me?"

"I don't know. If the Devil finds out…"

"There's no chance he will. He forgot about me a long time ago."

"Ok, I'll get her."

Bakoth disappears, and I return to the house I've built here to prepare for the arrival of my guest.

CHAPTER THREE
EMMA

I put the finishing touches to my picture of the Moon and take a step back. It's perfect. For a moment, I'd considered adding in the man but changed my mind.

I think I must have been exhausted last night when looking through the telescope, and the dream was a manifestation of my tiredness as well. There's no chance of anyone living on the Moon, especially dressed in jeans and a t-shirt. They couldn't breathe. *Fact.* Anyway, my picture is perfect—a haze of reds, oranges and purples, surrounding the Moon as it rises in the night sky. A magical scene if ever I've seen one.

I throw my brushes into the sink. I'll clean them up in a bit. I need a cup of tea before I do anything else. I've been working on the painting for the last three hours and haven't stopped for a drink. I know it's bad for me—my aunt always tells me the same thing. I head over to the makeshift kitchen we have in the studio, and switching on the kettle to boil, I retrieve a clean cup from beside the sink. I grab an English breakfast tea bag from a box of assorted flavors and pop it in the cup. The kettle boils, and I finish my tea off with a splash of milk. I love a *builders brew,* nice and strong. I take the first sip while I stand and admire my painting.

"Dralran will be pissed off you didn't put him in it," a deep voice comes from behind me.

The cup drops out of my hands and smashes on the floor, sending hot tea over my feet. I'm not sure whether to scream because of the intruder or because my feet now feel like they're on fire.

"Sorry about that, I didn't mean to scare you."

Spinning around, I make my decision on what to scream about. A mountain of a man stands in front of me, and I know instantly he's not human—the fact his eyes are glowing orange, and he has horns on his head kind of give it away.

Without another moment's hesitation, I speed off through the building, heading for the front door.

"Why do they always run?" I hear from behind me.

My life can't get any weirder at the moment—a man on the moon and a strange creature in the art studio. I think either someone's been covertly giving me drugs or I've finally lost it. I get to the door and reach out for the handle, but I don't have a chance to grab hold of it before a large arm wraps itself around my waist and pulls me toward an even harder body. This is it. This is the moment I die or worse. Oh god, please no, haven't I been through enough in my life?

"Please don't hurt me," I implore desperately.

"I'm not here to hurt you, don't worry. I'm just the delivery boy."

The man pulls me even closer to him.

"Delivery boy?" I'm not sure I like the sound of that.

Kicking my legs out, I try my hardest to escape, but it's futile. I've no strength against this man, thing, demon…whatever he, it, is.

"Let me go?" I try one more time to break free, but the world around me starts to blur.

"Hold tight, Emma. Things are about to get a little crazy," the thing holding me warns, and he's not wrong.

Turning around in circles, the decor of the art gallery disappears. I feel sick and shut my eyes.

Is this death? Am I dying? Is that what's happening? Am I going to Hell? I must be. I didn't think I'd been evil in my life. I've always tried to do the right thing. I know I ran over a bird once although I tried to avoid it. I even crashed my car trying to miss it. That must be it...I'm a murderer. I took the life of one of God's creatures, and now I'm dying, I don't deserve to go to Heaven. I hope Hell won't be too bad. Who am I kidding? It's Hell. It's going to be the worst place in the entire universe. I did bury the bird so it wouldn't get eaten by a fox, but I did it in my back garden. I should have done it on consecrated ground—that's what I did wrong. Maybe I can reason with the Devil? Oh, God, I don't want to die yet, and I definitely don't want to go to Hell.

"You're not dead." A deep voice, which doesn't belong to the man thing who brought me here, freezes my thoughts. I must have spoken the part about dying out loud. "You can open your eyes now, Emma. You might feel dizzy for a bit longer, but I can assure you the view is perfect."

"I don't want to look," I answer back, terrified of the fiery pits of Hell I'm about to see. I once did a painting of the underworld. It scared the crap out of me but made the biggest profit at my exhibition.

"I think you'll be pleasantly surprised when you do?"

The voice is urging me to trust him. I'm not stupid, though. It's all part of the plan—lure me into a false sense of security, and then bang, throw me into a fire and burn half my skin away. I won't fall for it.

Stretching my arms out in front of me, I stumble blindly forward. The ground is uneven, and I suddenly realize I don't feel hot. I always thought Hell would be as hot as, well, Hell. There isn't much screaming either, only silence and a repetitive noise that's eerie in its make-up. It sounds familiar—something I've heard before. But I can't place it.

"Why isn't there lots of screaming?" I ask the question to no one in particular.

I'm reluctant to open my eyes, so I have no idea if the person with the deep voice is still there.

"Why would there be screaming?" he responds from beside me. "Be careful, there's a big rock in front of you."

Too late...I smack my knees into it.

"Fuck." I shout out, and it echoes around me.

I know I'm going to need to check whether I've ripped my kneecap off or something. Maybe that's how torture works in Hell. I'm going to spend eternity in purgatory, walking around blindly and battering myself. It's a cop out if you ask me—lazy ass demons. Against my better judgement, I open my eyes slowly, prepared to be blinded by red, orange, and yellow flames. Instead, I am met with a vision of black night and stars, so many stars. I look down at my feet, gray rock, then I dare to look up. My head spins as I realize just where I am. Oh my God, it can't be…in the distance, I can see the Earth.

"Holy fuck, I'm on the Moon," I manage to spit out before my whole world goes black.

CHAPTER FOUR
DRALRAN

"She's a strange one?"

Bakoth stares down at Emma as she lays in my arms—I managed to catch her as she fell. I don't know where she believed my friend had brought her, but I suspect it wasn't anywhere good. Holding her closer, I carry her into my house. She doesn't wake when I move her, so I place her on the bed and pull the surrounding covers over her and tuck them in neatly.

When she arrived here with my friend, I used my magic to give her the ability to breathe without the need to wear one of those curious looking outfits the male humans used when they landed on the Moon.

Bakoth has followed me into the bedroom, but I usher him out.

"She's not strange. She's in shock. I'll let her rest for a while and then explain everything to her."

"Good luck with that. It's going to be an interesting talk…So, Emma, I live on the Moon because the Devil banished me from Hell for fucking his daughter."

I glare daggers at him. "I might leave that part out if it's all the same with you. She doesn't need to know what I got up to five hundred years ago."

"Man, such a long time. Does your dick still work?"

"Bakoth," I growl in warning.

A fiery ball appears in my hand, and I send it into the fire I prepared earlier, knowing Emma would be cold up here in space at first.

"Perfectly valid question, Dral. If my dick stopped working, I think I'd jump into the River Styx."

"Don't worry, I'll be there to push you in." I smirk.

Despite being stuck up here, Bakoth and I have remained firm friends. I think he's the reason I've made it through my banishment as well as I have.

"Yeah right, like you could take me in a fight."

Bakoth thumps me on the back. His superior strength sends me flying across the room, and I'm not a small man. There isn't much to do on the Moon except work out and watch. Although there have been certain points in human history when I walked away from watching. We're supposed to be the demons, filled with darkness, but there have been and still are some rulers in some countries who show us up. At least, when they die, I get to watch them receive their punishment, courtesy of Satan.

"I'm going to head off now." Bakoth looks down at Hell. "There's nothing else you need from me is there?"

I shake my head.

"No, that's just about it for the moment. If you could bring some food back in a few days, that'll be great. Emma's favorite dish is pasta with pesto sauce. If you can get the ingredients for it, even better. The recipe she uses was her mother's—it's in the cabinet next to the fridge in her house. You should probably make it seem like she's gone on holiday as well. Pack some of her clothes and belongings. You can bring them up here. We don't want anybody asking questions about her sudden disappearance."

"Probably not the best idea. Especially if Satan gets wind of it."

Bakoth and I slap hands together in a manly gesture of parting, and he disappears into thin air. I return to the bedroom to sit and wait for Emma to wake up.

It doesn't take long. She stretches and yawns as though she's stirring from a long slumber. The room is nice and warm, so it's probably lulled her into feeling comfortable and safe.

"Can I get you a drink?" I ask in a soft voice as she rolls over onto her other side.

She sits bolt upright in the bed, her eyes wide open.

"I'm on the Moon!"

Quickly scrambling from the bed, she opens the curtains, which I'd drawn earlier to help keep the room warm, and stares out for a few seconds before turning to face me. "I'm on the fucking Moon."

"You are."

I smile sweetly back at the terrified woman in front of me. Is it wrong my dick hardens in my jeans? She's so pretty even with her eyes as wide as saucers and her hands clasped protectively in front of her.

"How am I breathing?" She gasps as if she's trying to get air into her lungs, which is actually already there. "I need a spacesuit."

"No you don't. You're here with me, and I'm helping you breathe with magic."

"Magic doesn't exist," she responds in disbelief.

"Of course it does. You're on the Moon."

"Of course it does. I'm on the Moon," she repeats and then leans over and gasps again. "The Moon, not the Earth. I'm on the Moon—I'm miles and miles away from the Earth."

"Two hundred and thirty-eight thousand, eight hundred and fifty-five miles to be precise," I inform her helpfully.

I know her love of space. I saw the posters she had on her walls as she was growing up. All her artwork involves depictions of the universe in one way or another.

She opens her mouth to say something, but nothing comes out. Instead, I have to race forward as she faints again. I lay her out on the bed once more, but it doesn't take her as long to revive this time.

"How?" she asks as she stares at me. "How is this even possible?"

"I told you, magic."

"So you're a wizard, like Dumbledore?"

I can't help laughing. Harry Potter wizards are all humans know. I'm not sure what Emma would think if she knew Hogwarts existed for real. I'll save that particular fact for another day.

"No, I'm not a wizard. I'm a demon."

"But you look normal and don't have horns."

Emma cocks her head to the side, presumably checking for any traces of spikes.

"We don't all have horns. Bakoth is a strength demon. His kind have the small horns you saw. I'm a fire breathing demon. My powers come from the ability to control flames either with my hands or to shoot them from my mouth if I'm in a terrible mood."

"Are you in that kind of a mood today?"

"No, not at all. I'm so happy to have you here."

"Why am I here?"

Emma still clasps her hands tightly together in her lap as I watch her. Her fingers are covered in the colors of her artwork, but her nails are painted black with gold glitter to symbolize the stars, no doubt.

"Because I brought you here. Well, technically Bakoth brought you here, but I asked him to."

"My head hurts." She un-clenches her fists and rubs at her temples. "I don't think I understand any of this."

"It might take a few days to adjust to your new life, but I wouldn't worry about it. I'll be here to help you. I know how much you love the stars, so we can watch them together. It's a lot easier to see them up here, and you get a much better look at the planets as well. It's amazing watching Earth. There are so many humans with interesting characters. You can even nose into people's bedrooms. Some funny things go on when people don't think anyone else is watching."

Emma slides herself from the bed again and heads toward the door of the bedroom. I follow her, my hands in my pockets. My dick is still hard, but I'm trying to keep it adjusted so I don't scare her. I don't want her to worry too much at first about the physical side of her future. I'm not that evil. I know it's going to be an adjustment living on the Moon when she's used to Earth and all the people and noise down there. The silence up here will be deafening at first. It was for me, but at least she has me to guide her through it all.

"Adjust to my new life? What the hell are you on about?" she questions.

"Your new life here with me on the Moon."

Emma steps out of the bedroom and through the house toward the front door.

"On the Moon? Ok, I'm guessing the drugs have really kicked in now. Either that or I'm going to wake up in a straitjacket anytime soon," she mutters while standing by the front door and then she pinches herself. "Ouch." She looks at me with her brows furrowed together. "This is real, isn't it?"

"If I say yes, are you going to faint again?"

She shakes her head, no.

"Open the door and look out. That will give you the answers you seek."

"I'm scared."

"Why?"

"Because..."

"Because what?" I move closer to her, and she allows me to take her hand. It's cold and small in mine. She shivers, and I pull her into my arms. There's an actual fire burning within me, so I'm always hot.

"Because this can't be real."

I push the door open and lead her out across the dark side of the Moon to a position where she can see the Earth sitting in space. She gasps.

"It can't be real."

"It is. That's the Earth."

When I gaze into her eyes, I see the reflection of her planet in them. Her pupils are fully dilated with the shock of what she's seeing, She can't seem to look away from the view.

"It's beautiful. No, that's not the word for it. I don't think there is one," she says in awe.

I point to where dark clouds are gathering.

"That's over Mexico. It's a small storm. The hurricane they had there a few years ago was amazing to watch. The speed at which the clouds built and moved was something even I'd not witnessed before."

"Why me?"

Emma shifts in my arms to face me.

"Because since the day you were born, you've been mine to protect."

Tears tumble down her face, and she pulls away from me and runs. Where is she going? I don't think even she knows. There's no escape from the Moon without teleportation or a spaceship, neither of which are available to her.

She's always been mine, and finally, she's here.

CHAPTER FIVE
EMMA

I'm on the Moon, the Moon, the Moon—the ball of rock orbiting the Earth. I can see the planet I've lived on for thirty years from where I'm standing. It's big and round, filling the black sky. I can even see the sun from here although I'm not going to look directly at it.

This is real. I've not been drugged or gone mad. I know what I'm seeing is the truth. I don't know how I know, but I just do.

Why me?

I look behind me and see the man watching me from nearby.

"How long have you been here?"

"On the Moon or alive?"

"Both I guess."

"I'm seven hundred years old, and I've been on the Moon for five hundred years. Satan took offense to something I did and decided it would be better if I left Hell for a while. He's not come back for me yet."

"Seven hundred, Moon, five hundred, Satan, Hell," I repeat in shock.

The man smirks at me, and my body warms at the sight. How is it I feel I know him, even though I don't? Yeah, that'll probably be because you imagined him going down on you the other night after seeing him waving to you from the Moon, which incidentally, you are now standing on. My cheeks blush.

"The other night, I saw you in my dream."

"It wasn't a dream. It was a magical projection. It's why it felt so real."

The man moves closer to me, and I take a few steps back over the rocky ground.

"I think it's best if you keep your magical projections to yourself from now on."

"They might help you relax."

The man winks and smirks lustfully at me. His eyes sparkle with desire, and I haven't failed to notice the huge bulge in his jeans.

"I don't even know your name?"

"Dralran, but my friends call me Dral."

"Dralran. Does it have a meaning?"

"He who breathes fire," he says with a laugh. I can tell he's teasing me. "Does Emma have a meaning, then?"

"It does actually. It's derived from the German word Ermen and means universal."

Dral leans against a nearby rock with his muscular arms crossed over his chest. I try not to look at them, but then my eyes start to drift lower to the evidence of his desire, and I blush.

"Great name. My eyes are up here by the way."

I fluster, and turning around, I gaze out into infinity. There's nothing else here to look at except darkness, planets, and stars.

"Why me? Why have you brought me here?" I gesture wide with my hands.

I still can't believe what I'm actually seeing. Am I the first human to walk in space without the aid of breathing equipment?

"Because you're going to be my wife," Dral replies in a matter of fact voice. I can't help laughing. "What's so funny, Emma?"

Spinning back around, I turn to face him. He's classically handsome with his square jawline and perfect features framed by his long hair. His eyes pierce me to the spot. He's admitted he's a demon, but if I didn't know better, I'd say he's more like an angel sent to protect me.

"Let me get this straight. The Devil has banished you to live on the Moon. I'm thirty years old. You're at least seven hundred. I'm going to be your wife." I've started repeating his words again. "I'm not sure if this is a nightmare or insanity."

"It's your new reality, Emma. I know you much better than you think, and you know me as well. I've been with you since birth. I've watched you throughout your life, and I've seen everything you've done."

"That's not helping. It's just plain creepy."

"As my wife I'll give you everything you want."

"You live on the Moon," I remind him.

"It doesn't matter as long as we're together."

"I can't do this." I start to hyperventilate.

Dralran pushes off his rock and comes over to rub my back

"Remember your parents' funeral. You thought you'd never get through it, but you did. I was watching you the entire time. The pain you had to bear was far greater than it should have been for someone your age. I wanted to stand there and hold your hand to support you, but I couldn't. All I could do was wrap my spirit around you and give you as much strength as I could. I hated seeing you so broken. It nearly broke me as well."

I move so I can settle in his arms. I don't know why. This should be freaking me out, but I remember the day of my parents' funeral too vividly. I knew someone had been with me that day. I thought it was the ghosts of my parents, but now I know it was Dral.

"So you've been watching me since I was born?"

"Since that very moment," he confirms.

It sounds a little creepy. Well, a lot creepy actually, but I need to know more. I've never felt alone in my life. It's always seemed like someone has been with me, and I'm starting to understand why.

"Do you remember the time you got really scared walking home one night because you thought someone was following you?" Dral asks.

"Which time? I'm always scared going home on my own in the dark."

"The time when you fell and scraped your knee."

"That was a few years ago."

"I know, but I remember it well. There was someone following you that night. He'd already killed several women. I wasn't going to allow him to hurt you. I sent Bakoth to Earth to protect you. The serial killer's in Hell now. Just where he deserves to be."

I look up at him, my eyes going wide.

"Ok, that anecdote's not just freaked me out completely!"

"You do seem to have a knack for getting into trouble. I remember the time you turned on the gas stove but didn't ignite it. You got an idea for a painting and just wandered off. Thankfully, I could use my power of fire to ignite it before you blew both your home and yourself up."

"I don't remember that."

"I don't think you know half the stuff I've helped you with and protected you from. Do you recall your imaginary friend as a child?"

We start to walk back to the house together. He wraps his arm around my shoulders and guides me over the rocks.

"I didn't have an imaginary friend."

"Yes, you did. It was me. We used to talk for hours. I was sad the day I knew it was time for you to grow up and lose me."

"I'm sorry, but you know this really does sound creepy."

"Meh, I'm not sorry. I was the friend you needed as a child, and I'll be the lover you need as an adult."

"Ok, you need to stop saying this. I'm not staying here."

"You do realize you've no choice in the matter?

There's no way to return to Earth unless I get Bakoth to take you."

"I'll go and stand where I know someone with a telescope can see me and wave. They'll send a spaceship for me."

"That won't work. You're cloaked by magic to prevent anyone seeing you."

He pushes the door open to his home and allows me to walk in first.

"You can't do this."

"I can, and I have?"

"What about my friends?"

"We can send Leah a note to let her know you're happy and safe."

"She'll want to know where I am."

I place my hands angrily on my hips as I stand in the middle of his lounge.

"I'm afraid we can't tell her, but I'm sure she'll believe it if you say a millionaire whisked you away to his hidden island for all the sex you can get."

"No, she'll immediately think I've been kidnapped and report it to the police. They'll search for me and confirm I've been taken, and when they don't find me, everyone I know will conclude that I'm dead and cry."

"I'll think about it. We can't tell her the truth. She

works for the space agency. It would be too dangerous."

"Ugh." I throw my hands up into the air and stomp off toward the kitchen. Then a thought hits me, and I halt, frozen to the spot. I turn around slowly. I can feel my cheeks burning bright red again. "You said you watch me all the time. Do you mean when I'm sleeping?"

"Of course. Sometimes you have dreams about the accident. I like to soothe you."

"You watch me in the shower?"

"I must admit I've had some great orgasms watching you shower." I feel my body heat up. I don't know whether to be freaked out anymore or climb him and hump him. This man knows me better than I know myself. "My favorite times are when you pleasure yourself while you're in there. Watching the water and your fingers between your thighs as you let out your little moans. I also approve of the vibrator you have. It will have prepared you for when I put my dick inside you."

"Oh God." I want to die of embarrassment. Seriously, he's watched me masturbating. Another recollection hits me. It's even more cringeworthy. "Did you watch me when I…" I cough into my hand, struggling to find the words I need to finish my sentence. "When I…"

"Had sex?" Dral's face darkens, and I can tell he's angry. "Yes, I saw that. You really did pick the wrong bloke to have your first time with. He was useless, and I know you faked your orgasm. It was obvious. I've seen the real ones you've given yourself."

"You don't know that," I try to argue, but Dral raises a knowing eyebrow at me. "Ok but it's difficult for a woman to orgasm on their first sexual encounter because it can be painful."

"Not if it's with the right man. I'll show you how it's done properly, and we'll have the rest of our lives to make sure you get as many orgasms as you can."

I sigh heavily at this further reference to me staying here. Dral may know me, but I don't know him. He's a demon. I didn't even know they existed when I got up this morning. He breathes fire. He's from Hell. Hell!

"I can't stay here, Dral. You may know me, but I don't know you."

"That's not true."

He takes a seat on the sofa while I remain standing by the kitchen door.

"I didn't even know you existed until I saw you wave at me."

"You do know me. Think about your art, your passions, you're favorite colors."

I shut my eyes and look into my mind to confirm what he's saying.

"My pictures are of the Moon and Hell. I am fascinated with space and the universe. I love the colors of fire—vivid oranges, reds, and yellows."

"They're all me, Emma."

"The feeling of being protected...as though someone was caring for me and looking out for me, even when it seemed the world was conspiring against me."

"Me."

Everything begins to make sense. I realize Dral has always been a part of me, and I've loved him before I even knew he existed. He's me and I'm him. Something powerful exists between us.

"I was banished here for sleeping with the Devil's daughter. But from the first time I saw you, I knew that wasn't the reason why I was sent here. It was because of you. Fate intervened and gave us to each other."

I take a long breath to fill my lungs and walk past him and head outside again. It doesn't take me long to reach a point where I can see the Earth. The colors are so vibrant, and it's so big. Dral appears behind me. He wraps his arms around my waist.

"You can never leave the Moon?" I question.

"No, I'm banished here for eternity."

"Ok."

"I can't let you go back to Earth without me."

Dral kisses my cheek and then down over my neck. It feels familiar, and I relax into it. He scoops me up in his arms and carries me back to the house.

"I'll stay on one condition."

"What is it?"

"Bakoth has to bring my art equipment up here. I need to paint this view of the Earth."

CHAPTER SIX
DRALRAN

"Anything for you," I tell Emma as I enter the bedroom with her and lower her onto the bed.

She bites her lip and looks up at me with hooded eyelids. My dick hardens so much I swear the zipper of my jeans will have left an imprint on it.

"Wow, the whole Moon is my home. I'll be richer than Jeff Bezos."

I can't help laughing at her response.

"You do know he's a demon right? He couldn't get that many people to do his bidding if he wasn't."

Emma sits up. The seductive look in her eyes has gone.

"So there are more demons on Earth? Who are they? Please, you have to tell me. Seriously, half of the

British parliament must be because I've never known so many people to make so many disastrous decisions. What about the royal family? I could see the Queen as a werewolf or something. She does love to hunt."

I lower my body over hers and push her back against the bed.

"Enough with the questions. It's been five hundred years since I last had sex, and since you turned eighteen, I've been tortured by your sexy body every day. I need inside you. I'll answer everything later."

I press a kiss against her lips.

"I'm not that easy you know? We should at least date before we fuck."

"Make love," I growl. "And we have dated. Every time you've watched a movie with popcorn, I've sat beside you, watching it with you. Every time you've gone for a run in the park, wearing your tight little shorts, I've been there with you, making sure you're safe. Every time you've been to a drive-through, then sat in the car eating your meal by yourself and talking to nobody in particular, I've been beside you, eating my own meal and answering your questions."

"You make me sound so sad."

I kiss her cheeks and down her neck.

"No, not sad. I know you could hear my answers to the questions in your head. I've always been there."

"So when I asked myself, 'Should I wear the pink or purple blouse for my opening show?' You answered…"

Emma trails her hands over my shoulders and then down my back.

"Always pink."

"And that's what I wore."

"It matches your complexion perfectly."

"And when I asked myself, 'What should I paint next?' You answered…"

"The Moon," we both say simultaneously.

I reach down and find the bottom hem of Emma's top. Pulling it gently up and over her head, I reveal her breasts to me for the first time in reality.

"Where shall I go on holiday this year?" Emma continues with the questions she knows the answers to.

"You ignored my advice on that one."

"Scotland was lovely."

"I know, but it rained most of the time you were there. You weren't able to get as many paintings done as you wanted to, so you wished you'd chosen Santorini like I suggested."

"Maybe I can paint it from up here instead."

"You can paint whatever you want to from up here. You just need the Earth to be on the right axis."

"I can see Australia?"

Emma runs her hands through my hair as I reach behind her and remove her bra. I instantly take one of her pert nipples into my mouth and suck on the tender nub.

"You just have to wait until it's bedtime in the UK."

"I'm going to like living here with you."

"Good, I'm enjoying you living here already. It's so much better than doing this to you in your dreams. Your scent is even more intoxicating in person. Your heat, warmer, and your skin, softer."

"I have to say it's much better knowing your lips and hands on me are real and not part of a dream."

I pull Emma's jeans down her svelte thighs and throw them onto the bedroom floor. She won't be needing them for a while. Her underwear follows the same path, and my mouth goes straight to her pussy. I've waited since she turned eighteen to taste her. The previous four hundred and eighty-eight years of sexual frustration were nothing compared to the last twelve. They have been the longest years of my life. I knew it had to be the right time to bring her here, though. She had to be able to understand my life, and at thirty, she's mature enough to do so now. She's a perfect match for me. I wasn't joking when I said we'd dated. We've been together more than she can ever imagine. But it's only now it can be physical.

I lick the length of her slit and savor the taste. It's even better than I imagined, sweet and pure. Nothing like the demons I've been with. There is an innocence about Emma, even though I know she's not a virgin. How I didn't kill the guy who took her virginity, I don't know. Well I do. I was stuck on the Moon. Bakoth told me the guy had to live with his failure as a lover, and he assured me that would be a worse torture than burning him alive. He was right. I've looked in on another couple of relationships he's been in and all the women fake it with him. I couldn't be happier.

"Dral," Emma purrs as I push my tongue inside her and wet her opening ready for my cock. I'm still fully clothed, and my cock is begging to be released. Sitting up, I pull my t-shirt over my head and lower my hand back to her pussy. I push one finger and then another inside her. She squirms while at the same time trying to get a good look at my torso. Thankfully, exercise has been my biggest friend on the Moon, and in terms of human age, I'm only a couple of years older than Emma when you consider the whole demon thing. The thought of the future and her aging hits me momentarily, but I push it aside. That will be something I'll have to figure out later. For now, I need inside her. Pulling my fingers from her warmth. I step off the bed and lower my jeans.

"Holy fuck. I thought you were big, but I didn't realize how big."

"Pure demon," I tease and position myself at her entrance. I can't wait any longer to have her.

"Wait." She pushes against my chest. "Protection. I'm not on the pill. What happens? Does it all work the same way as humans?"

She looks down between us. On the outside, I look like a human, but my demon half is on the inside. My veins are full of fire not blood.

"Does it matter?"

"I don't know if I'm ready for children yet. I mean, I've just found out I'm spending the rest of my life living on the Moon with a demon." She places her hands over her eyes. "I want children, but...."

I remove her hands from her face and place them down at her side.

"I'll make sure you don't get pregnant today. Answering your question, it doesn't work the same way. I can choose to release my essence into you or not. Inside you'll still experience my fire."

"Fire!" she exclaims fearfully.

"Wait and see." I push inside her without further discussion or warning.

My entire body ignites with satisfaction. I'm finally achieving the lifelong ambition I didn't know I had until recently. I've found my soulmate, and I'm never going to stop worshipping her. I settle myself deep inside Emma and allow her to relax around me. I know her first time was the only time she's been with a man, and he wasn't really much of a man.

"Feel. Full," she moans. "Need." Every word is punctuated with desperate gasps. I know exactly what she needs, and I withdraw and then slam back into her. This isn't just a pussy I'm burying my dick into… it's my pussy.

My home.

My sanctuary.

My savior.

"Dral," Emma murmurs as she moves her hands from her sides and digs them into the flesh on my back.

Her nails scratch marks down my flawless skin. She's marking me as her own as well. She doesn't know how many times she's done this to me in her sleep before. How I've held her as she sobbed for the loss of her parents. I hated Fate that day. I cursed the

Devil. I pleaded with Destiny to allow me to be the one to torture the drunk driver who slammed into their car, but I wasn't permitted. I now understand why, because if Destiny had granted my request, I would have truly turned evil and not been the demon, no, the man, Emma needed.

My hips buck wildly as I take Emma hard and fast now. Both of us need this. Our mouths and our tongues twist together in a passionate dance of lust and love. I taste her, and she devours me. My orgasm builds, and as promised, I hold back the part of me which would instantly fill her with our child, but I allow the heat of my fire to descend from my balls and down my shaft. As it erupts inside her, my release burns through my body. Emma's eyes go wide as she feels the heat inside her, and she clamps down on my length in a powerful orgasm of her own. She milks everything I have to give her. I'm hot. She's cold. Together we're the perfect temperature. Eventually, my high recedes, and I gently withdraw from her and lay beside her. Pulling her close to me.

"What the hell was that?"

"My love."

"It was hot!"

"It always will be." I press a kiss to the top of her

forehead but stop when thick, black smoke fills the room. Shit!

There is only one person who makes an entrance like that...

Satan.

CHAPTER SEVEN
EMMA

I'm struggling to catch my breath from the lovemaking with Dral when the air around us fills with smoke.

"What's happening?" I press my body closer into him. "Is this part of what happens after you have sex with someone? I know it was smoking hot, but you don't need to set the house on fire."

"I wish it were me." Dral jumps from the bed and searches for his jeans as the smoke continues to thicken. "I need you to stay calm, ok? You're about to meet someone who may scare you a little bit."

"Scare me? Who? I've just slept with a demon, and I'm on the Moon. What could be scarier?"

"I can." A big booming voice fills the room.

My mouth falls open as I look at the entity who's

appeared in front of me. He's red all over with eyes as black as the night.

"My liege, please. She's an innocent." Dral bows to the intruder in our bedroom.

Liege?

Who would Dral call that?

Why would he be so scared?

It dawns on me.

Crap.

This must be the Devil.

And he's pissed off I've slept with a demon.

Can my day get any worse?

Seriously, why did I bother burying that bird?

I was destined for Hell all along.

I should have done all the bad things: smoking, drinking, stealing, and sleeping around. No, I don't think I would have liked the last one. Dral is man enough, no, demon enough for me in my dreams and in real life.

Emma, stop talking to yourself. The devil is standing in front of you, and he's mad. You need to get up and bow to him or something.

I can hear Dral's thoughts in my head. I spring from the bed, keeping the sheet around me and bow my head to the Devil.

Do I need to get lower down?

Maybe curtsy?

"Please, your…er…majesty, this is as much my fault as it is Dral's. I agreed to what we just did. He didn't force himself on me or anything."

I crouch down on the floor, hoping it's low enough to show deference to the fact he's the Devil! Fuck, Satan's in front of me, and I'm not dead yet! Or at least I don't think I am.

I so wanted to go to Heaven.

Damn sexy demons with their big dicks.

"Does she ever stop with the internal monologue?" Satan inquires.

"No, but I do find it endearing. At least, I know I'm hearing the truth," Dral responds but keeps his head lowered.

"W-What?" I stammer. "You're reading my thoughts."

Fuck you both.

Shit.

Sorry.

I didn't mean that. I know you're the Devil please don't burn me alive.

I'm young.

I'd like to experience a bit more of life.

Satan lets out a thunderous laugh.

"Finally. It had to happen Dral. You knew that

when I sent you here."

"What had to happen?" Dral raises his head and cocks an eyebrow at the Devil.

"You were so bored with the demon life you needed more—you needed love. I didn't think it would take you five hundred years to discover the truth and the one, but I'm sure it's just Fate messing around and trying to annoy me again by not giving you Emma sooner."

I'm still frozen to the spot as the Devil loses the red color to his skin, and his eyes return to those of a human. I can't help thinking that he does actually look like the guy from the television show named after him.

Hmm, nice.

Dral turns and growls at me. "Don't even think about it. You're mine."

"Stop reading my thoughts," I retort and put my hand on my hip.

The sheet falls to my waist, and I quickly grab it to cover myself.

"Thank you for appreciating my true form, but alas, I'm a happily married demon." Satan winks at me playfully.

"Well, I'm a one demon woman. But it doesn't mean I can't say you're cute."

"Damn well does." Dral huffs and folds his arms across his chest, "Are you going to send her back, my liege?" This time his face changes, and he looks genuinely worried.

"If I thought she was just a means for you to get off, then I would. But from the energy in the room, I can feel she's a lot more to you than that. I know generations of your family were torture demons, but it was never the right profession for you. You've always been a watcher and protector. Emma has become your profession, as strange as it sounds."

The Devil smiles warmly at us both, and I can't help thinking how un-demonic he is. There's genuine warmth and affection in his, dare I think it, friendship with Dralran.

"I can assure you, Emma, I have no friends, demon or otherwise," the Devil responds with a stern look. " You both now have a choice of which path to take. I don't think you're the sort of person to want to live in Hell, Emma."

I shake my head feverishly. No way, I don't want to go there. The thought of it scares the life out of me.

"It's not as wretched as humans say it is, by the way." Satan looks hurt at my vehemence.

"Do you torture people? Is there lots of screaming in pain?"

"Only in the lost souls part."

"Sorry, I think I'm more of a Heaven girl. I like peace and quiet so I can concentrate on painting."

"Ok, that leaves you with two options. You can stay here on the Moon, or you can both return to Earth. Dral, you know this means you'll be tying your life to Emma's? When she dies so will you."

"I've lived for seven hundred years. I don't want to spend another moment of my life without Emma."

Dral comes over to me and pulls me close to him. His body is still heated. He's like a radiator. I'll never be cold in winter again.

"What does it mean he'll be tied to me? Will he become human?" I have so many questions running through my head.

"No, he'll never be human. I can't take his powers away, only bind them like I've done with his ability to teleport. However, he knows he can't use them on Earth for fear of being caught, so I shall allow him to keep them intact."

"So he can't light the fire in my house by breathing on it or teleport me to the Seychelles for a luxury holiday without the whole getting on a plane part?"

"The fire, yes, as long as you are alone. The Seychelles is a little different. If nobody knows you are there, then I think I could overlook it as well."

"Damn, no five star luxury hotels then."

"A tent on a secluded beach would be your limit, I'm afraid. Questions could be raised about how you got there. It's too much of a risk." The Devil sighs sadly.

"I don't know. I can see some advantages to being together somewhere deserted." Dral winks and reaches around to pinch my bottom.

"Not in front of Satan," I scold him and push his hand away. Dral blows his lips out in frustration. "What about the Moon?"

"What about it?" Satan queries and looks out of the bedroom window to the dark universe beyond.

"Can we come back here?"

"Why?" Both Satan and Dral question simultaneously.

"Because it's the place I saw Dral first, the place I spoke to him first, and the place we consummated our love." The Moon has definitely grown on me. I won't see it the same ever again.

Smoke starts to swirl around the Devil's feet again. He's going to disappear any minute now. Will he give me an answer?

"Every year, on this day, you can return for a full twenty-four hours to the place where you were first together, here on the Moon. You can be alone, away from the vibrancy of the world below, and during that time you can remind each other of the love you share and the power you hold to watch over others." With those final words, the Devil disappears, and I'm left alone once again on the Moon with the man I was born to love.

"What do we do now? Will he send us back down to Earth?"

Dral shakes his head.

"No, he's returned my ability to teleport. I can feel it."

He reaches out and takes my hand.

"Do you want to go back to Earth now, Dral?"

I look out the window this time to where I know Earth sits in space on the lighter side of the Moon.

"How many hours do we have until midnight in the UK?" Dral asks.

"Two and a half. Why?"

"Because we still have two and a half hours for me to worship your body before we return to reality."

Dral lifts me up close to his body and pushes me against the bedroom wall. Then freeing himself from his jeans, he immediately thrusts inside me. I'm ready, willing, and waiting for him—my demon from beyond the Earth. Just as I always have been since the moment he started watching me.

ABOUT ANNA EDWARDS

Anna Edwards is a British author from the depths of the rural countryside near London. When she has some spare time, she can also be found writing poetry, baking cakes (and eating them), or behind a camera snapping like a mad paparazzo. She's an avid reader who turned to writing to combat her depression and anxiety. She has a love of traveling and likes to bring this to her stories to give them the air of reality. She likes her heroes hot and hunky with a dirty mouth, her heroines demure but with spunk, and her books full of dramatic suspense.

CONNECT WITH ANNA EDWARDS
www.AuthorAnnaEdwards.com
Newsletter: http://eepurl.com/cwxJ6v
Facebook, Friend: TheAuthorAnnaEdwards
Email: anna1000edwards@gmail.com

THE CONTROL SERIES

The Control Series: A complete, dramatic, witty, and sensual suspense romance set predominantly in London.

Surrendered Control

Divided Control

Misguided Control

Controlling Darkness

Controlling Heritage

Controlling Disgrace

Controlling Expectations

Controlling the Past

Also available:

The Control Series Boxset

THE GLACIAL BLOOD SERIES

A world of shifters and witches, magic and mayhem, unforgivable lies and unbreakable love. A world where family is born not only through blood, but bond. With plenty of the threats to come—and a secret that remains untold.

The Touch of Snow

Fighting the Lies

Fallen for Shame

Shattered Fears

Hidden Pain

Stolen Choices

A Deadly Affair

Power of a Myth - October 2020

Banishing Regrets - December 2020

The Touch of Snow	Fighting the Lies	Fallen for Shame
ANNA EDWARDS	ANNA EDWARDS	ANNA EDWARDS
Shattered Fears	Hidden Pain	Stolen Choices
ANNA EDWARDS	ANNA EDWARDS	ANNA EDWARDS
A Deadly Affair	The Power of a Myth	Banishing Regrets
ANNA EDWARDS	ANNA EDWARDS	ANNA EDWARDS

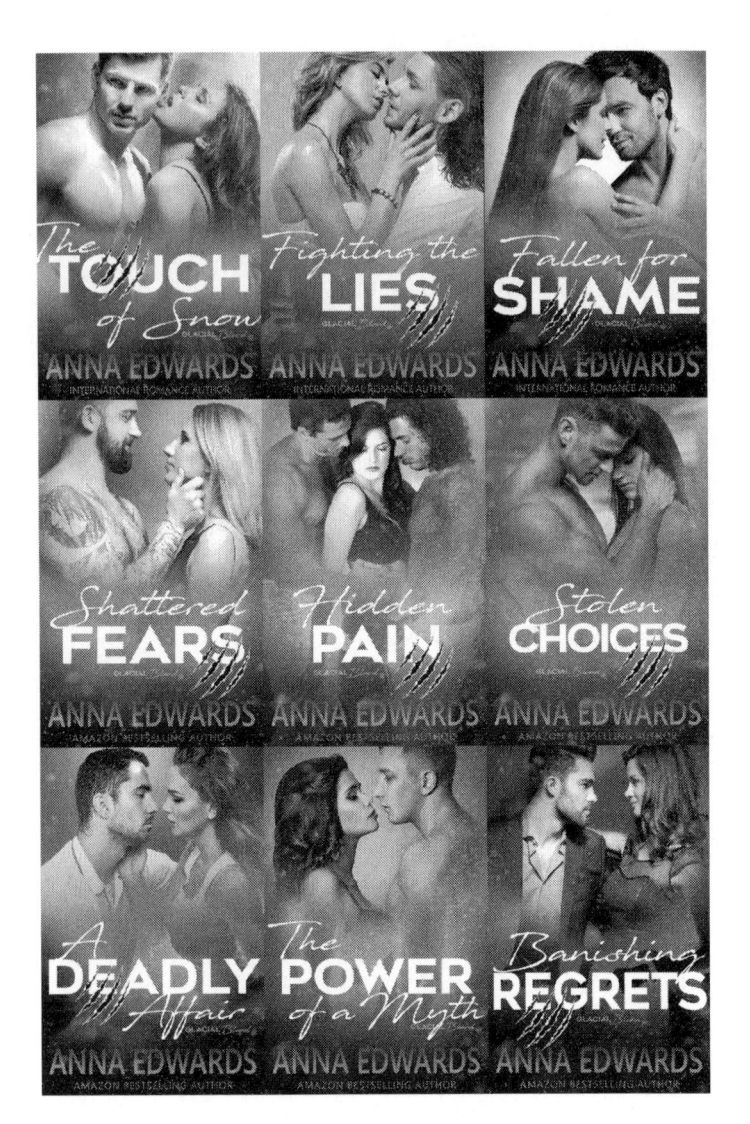

DARK SOVEREIGNTY SERIES

A complete dark and suspenseful series set amongst the elite of a London society intent on finding power in the wrong place.

Legacy of Succession

Tainted Reasoning

A Father's Insistence

SING WITH ME
SAVING TATE COLLECTION

Are you ready to meet the hottest new rock band on the planet?

Sing with Me by Anna Edwards, coming June 22nd

A With me In Seattle Universe Novel from Lady Boss Press.

Pre-order now

Amazon US: https://amzn.to/2X37NAy

Amazon UK: https://amzn.to/3bAvGog

Amazon CA: https://amzn.to/2WA4vWM

Amazon AU: https://amzn.to/3cDqQs2

Blurb:

Tate Gordon is the lead singer of Saving Tate, the hottest new rock band in Seattle. Having been mentored by music legends, Nash, for several years, the group are about to head out on their first world tour. Tate's excited, but he's struggling at the same time with the secrets he's been keeping. His friends don't know the truth about his youth or the confusion running through his head. Will Tate's past destroy everything the group have been working for when his past returns in a chance encounter?

Zoey Danson is a hot commodity in the record industry, and her boss wants her to travel with one of his top clients, Saving Tate, as they embark on their world tour. She's not entirely sure about being stuck on a tour bus with four famously horny men but mounting debts, thanks to her deadbeat mother, mean she doesn't have a choice.

When Zoey ascends the steps of the tour bus, looking hot and carrying a clip board with a full itinerary, sparks instantly fly between her and Tate. Can these two keep it professional, or will their instant attraction lead to an explosive disaster no one could have foreseen?

Sing with me is part of Kristen Proby's 'With me in Seattle' world and the start of a brand new rockstar romance series from the author, Anna Edwards.

The amazing summer launch lineup includes books from these AMAZING authors:

Melissa Brown

Anna Edwards

Bailie Hantam

Leigh Lennon

Stacey Lewis

Julie Prestsater

Jen Talty

Mary A. Wasowski

All of these stories stand alone, and are tied to the With Me In Seattle Universe in some way. You do not need to read them in any order.

https://www.ladybosspress.com/with-me-in-seattle

> I'm drowning in a sea of nothing, and this is an experience that will only come once in my lifetime.

ALSO BY ANNA EDWARDS

Beauty's War - Gods Reborn with Claire Marta

Apollo's Protection - Gods Reborn with Claire Marta

Oliver - Part of Blaire's World

Redemption - Book Ten of the Cavalieri Della Morte

Overexposed - A Skeleton Kings Prequel

Cruel Angels with Dani René

Happily Ever Crowned with Lexi C. Foss

Happily Ever Bitten with Lexi C. Foss

Frozen Sector

Zhànshì - Part of the Sinister Fairytales collection